PIANO • VOCAL • GUIT

DISNEY'S

# TEACHER'S PET

BASEMAN

# CONTENTS

ISBN 0-634-07741-4

**WALT DISNEY MUSIC COMPANY**

**WONDERLAND MUSIC COMPANY, INC.**

DISTRIBUTED BY

HAL•LEONARD®
CORPORATION
7777 W. BLUEMOUND RD. P.O. BOX 13819 MILWAUKEE, WI 53213

Visit Hal Leonard Online at
**www.halleonard.com**

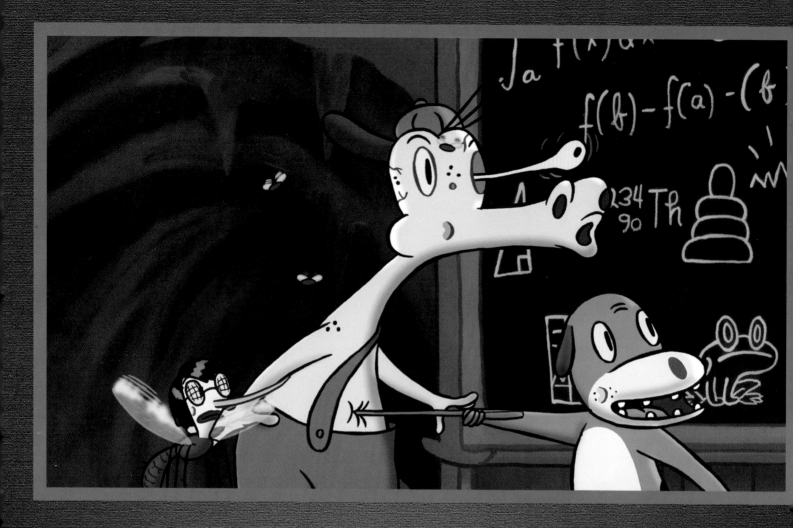

# TEACHER'S PET

Words and Music by
JOE LUBIN

# I WANNA BE A BOY
## (Teacher's Pet Theme)

Words and Music by BRIAN WOODBURY
and PETER LURYE

Moderately

22

Boy! _____
Dog! _____

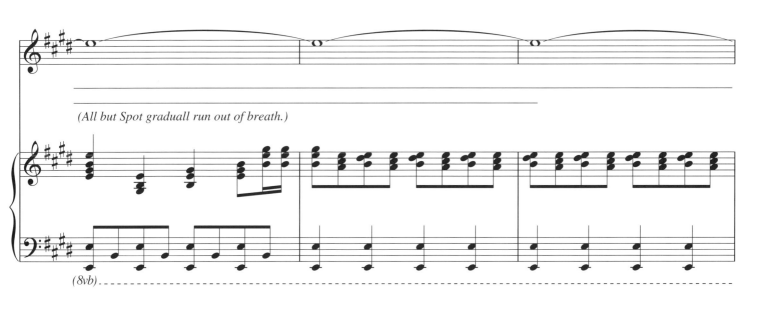

*(All but Spot graduall run out of breath.)*

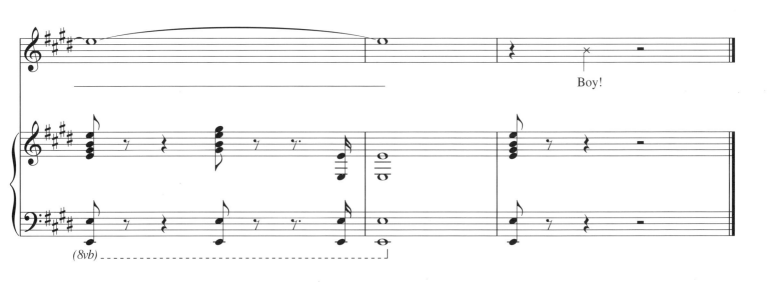

Boy!

# A BOY NEEDS A DOG

Words and Music by RANDY PETERSEN
and KEVIN QUINN

Slowly, expressively

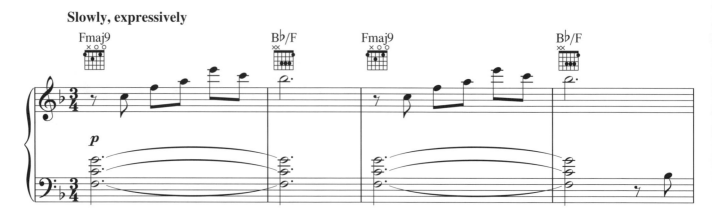

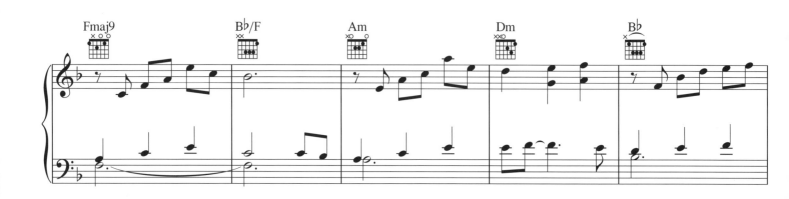

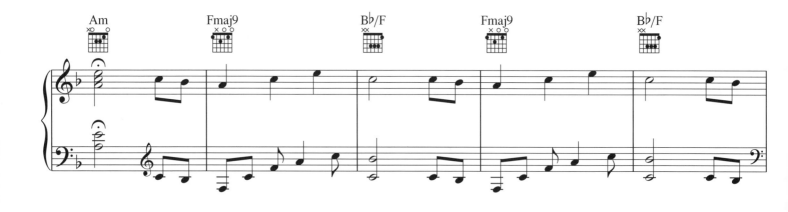

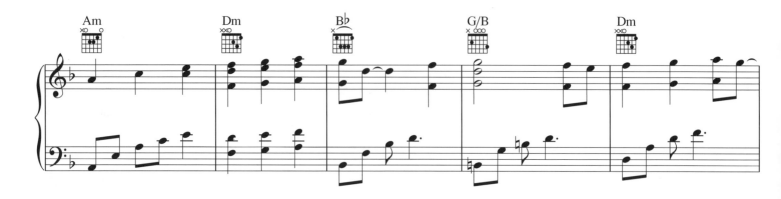

28

# A WHOLE BUNCH OF WORLD

Words by RANDY PETERSEN, KEVIN QUINN and CHERI STEINKELLNER
Music by RANDY PETERSEN and KEVIN QUINN

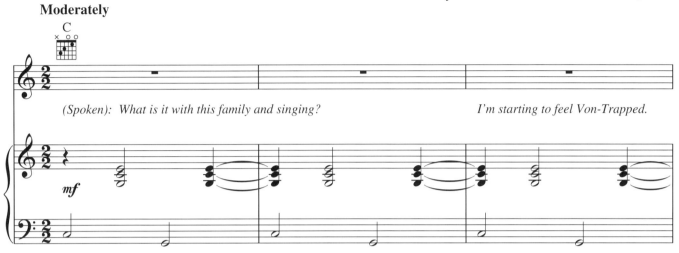

(Spoken): *What is it with this family and singing?*     *I'm starting to feel Von-Trapped.*

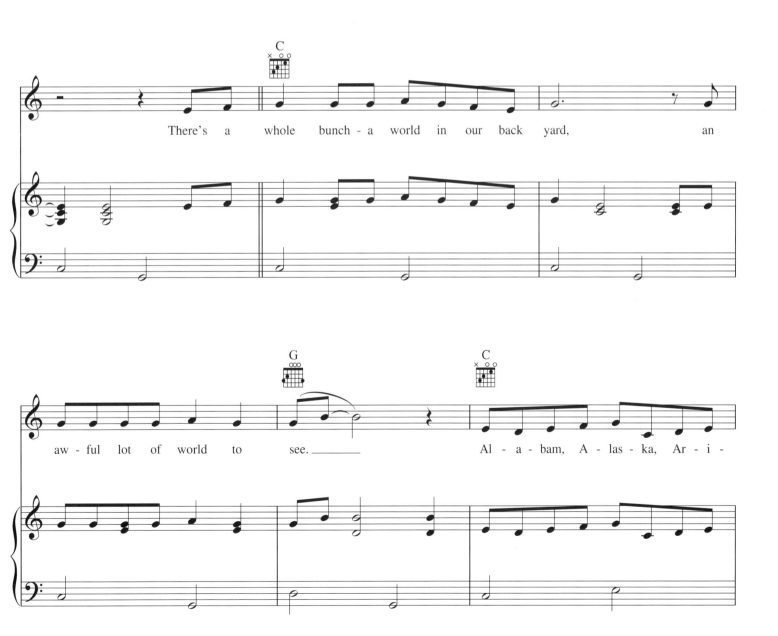

There's a whole bunch-a world in our back yard, an

aw-ful lot of world to see. _____ Al - a - bam, A - las - ka, Ar - i -

32

# SMALL BUT MIGHTY

Words and Music by RANDY PETERSEN
and KEVIN QUINN

# I, IVAN KRANK

Words by RANDY PETERSEN, KEVIN QUINN and CHERI STEINKELLNER
Music by RANDY PETERSEN and KEVIN QUINN

Moderate Tango

# TAKE THE MONEY AND RUN

Words by RANDY PETERSEN, KEVIN QUINN and CHERI STEINKELLNER
Music by RANDY PETERSEN and KEVIN QUINN

Lyrics:
mon - ey may be the root of all
*Saxophone solo ad lib.*

*Spoken:*
But it'll get you stuff / that is so close / to love, / that you won't know
pockets / to jingle. / / That's the way it is,

the difference.
I mean, you're single.

I love money.

I love my
(2.) Oh, cash!         I love cash!

1                                  2

*Want my wallet to be fat.*

(2.) Like the rest of me.

# I'M MOVIN' ON

Words by RANDY PETERSEN, KEVIN QUINN and CHERI STEINKELLNER
Music by RANDY PETERSEN and KEVIN QUINN

54

56

# A BOY NEEDS A DOG
## (Reprise)

Words and Music by RANDY PETERSEN
and KEVIN QUINN

game of leap-frog, a friend needs a friend; a

boy needs a dog. ___

**Moderately**

**Moderately fast**

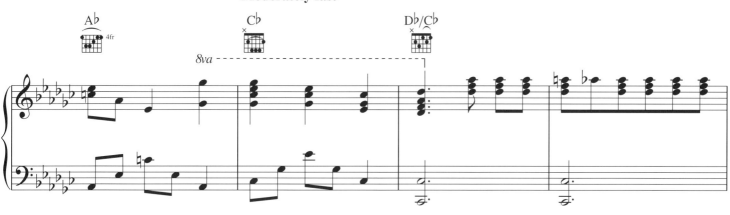

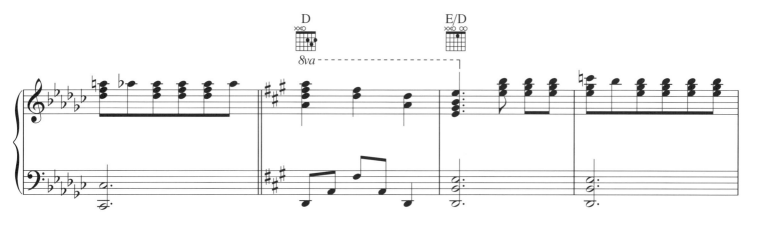

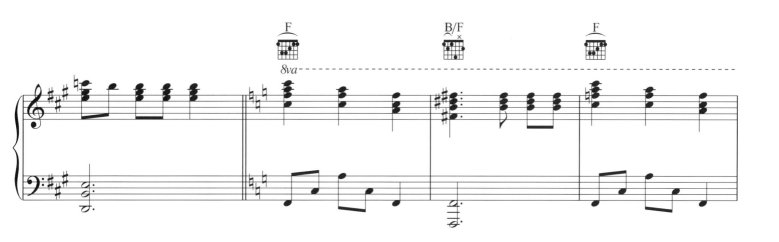

# PROUD TO BE A DOG

Words by BRIAN WOODBURY, PETER LURYE, RANDY PETERSEN,
KEVIN QUINN and CHERI STEINKELLNER
Music by BRIAN WOODBURY, PETER LURYE,
RANDY PETERSEN and KEVIN QUINN

68

**Moderately fast**

SPOT/GROUP I:                    dog!                    Needs a    dog!                    Needs a dog!                    Needs a

LEONARD/GROUP II: Needs a boy!                    Needs a boy!                    Needs a boy!

dog!          Dog!          Dog!     Dog!     Dog!     Dog!          Dog!_____

     Boy!     Boy!          Boy!     Boy!     Boy!     Boy!          Dog!_____